OWEN
ASTRONAUT

Level 6H

Written by Lucy George
Illustrated by Emma Foster
Reading Consultant: Betty Franchi

About Phonics

Spoken English uses more than 40 speech sounds. Each sound is called a *phoneme*. Some phonemes relate to a single letter (d-o-g) and others to combinations of letters (sh-ar-p). When a phoneme is written down, it is called a *grapheme*. Teaching these sounds, matching them to their written form, and sounding out words for reading is the basis of phonics.

Early phonics instruction gives children the tools to sound out, blend, and say the words without having to rely on memory or guesswork. This instruction gives children the confidence and ability to read unfamiliar words, helping them progress toward independent reading.

About the Consultant

Betty Franchi is an American educator with a Bachelor's Degree in Elementary and Middle Education as well as a Master's Degree in Special Education. Betty holds a National Boards for Professional Teaching Standards certification. Throughout her 24 years as a teacher, she has studied and developed an expertise in Phonetic Awareness and has implemented phonetic strategies, teaching many young children to read, including students with special needs.

Reading tips

This book focuses on two sounds made with the letters *ow*; (ŏ) as in c**ow** and (ō) as in bl**ow**.

Tricky and/or new words in this book

Any words in bold may have unusual spellings or are new and have not yet been introduced.

Tricky and/or new words in this book

mission position their colors pictures

Extra ways to have fun with this book

After the readers have read the story, ask them questions about what they have just read.

What colors were swirling in the black hole?
Can you remember two words that contain the different sounds shown by the letters ow?

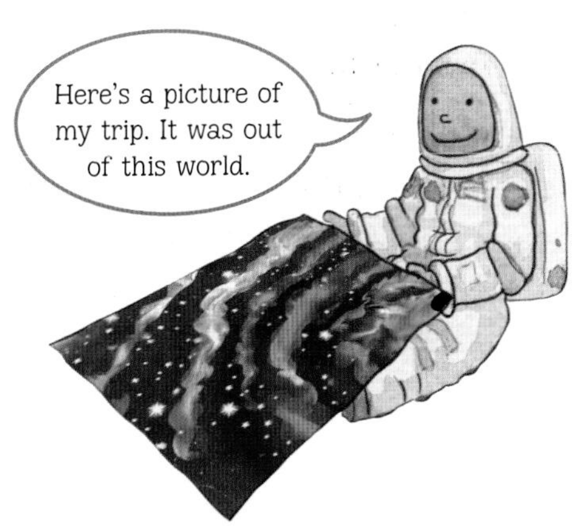

Here's a picture of my trip. It was out of this world.

A Pronunciation Guide

This grid contains the sounds used in the stories in levels 4, 5, and 6 and a guide on how to say them.

/ă/ as in p**a**t	**/ā/** as in p**ay**	**/âr/** as in c**ar**e	**/ä/** as in f**a**ther
/b/ as in **b**i**b**	**/ch/** as in **ch**ur**ch**	**/d/** as in **d**ee**d**/ mill**ed**	**/ĕ/** as in p**e**t
/ē/ as in b**ee**	**/f/** as in **f**i**f**e/ **ph**ase/ rou**gh**	**/g/** as in **g**a**g**	**/h/** as in **h**at
/hw/ as in **wh**ich	**/ĭ/** as in p**i**t	**/ī/** as in p**ie**/ b**y**	**/îr/** as in p**ier**
/j/ as in **j**u**dge**	**/k/** as in **k**i**ck**/ **c**at/ pi**qu**e	**/l/** as in **l**id/ needl**e** (nēd'l)	**/m/** as in **m**o**m**
/n/ as in **n**o/ sudd**en** (sŭd'n)	**/ng/** as in thi**ng**	**/ŏ/** as in p**o**t	**/ō/** as in t**oe**
/ô/ as in c**augh**t/ p**aw**/ f**o**r/ h**o**rrid/ h**oa**rse	**/oi/** as in n**oi**se	**/ʊ/** as in t**oo**k	**/ū/** as in c**u**te

/**ou**/ as in **ou**t	/**p**/ as in **p**o**p**	/**r**/ as in **r**oa**r**	/**s**/ as in **s**au**ce**
/**sh**/ as in **sh**ip/ di**sh**	/**t**/ as in **t**igh**t**/ stopp**ed**	/**th**/ as in **th**in	/**th**/ as in **th**is
/**ŭ**/ as in c**u**t	/**ûr**/ as in **ur**ge/ t**er**m/ f**ir**m/ w**or**d/ h**ear**d	/**v**/ as in **v**al**ve**	/**w**/ as in **w**ith
/**y**/ as in **y**es	/**z**/ as in **z**ebra/ **x**ylem	/**zh**/ as in vi**s**ion/ plea**s**ure/ gara**ge**/	/**ə**/ as in **a**bout/ it**e**m/ ed**i**ble/ gall**o**p/ circ**u**s
/**ər**/ as in butt**er**			

Be careful not to add an /uh/ sound to /s/, /t/, /p/, /c/, /h/, /r/, /m/, /d/, /g/, /l/, /f/ and /b/. For example, say /ff/ not /fuh/ and /sss/ not /suh/.

Owen the Astronaut is going on a **mission** to explore a black hole.

Its **position** is known, but what lies inside is unknown.

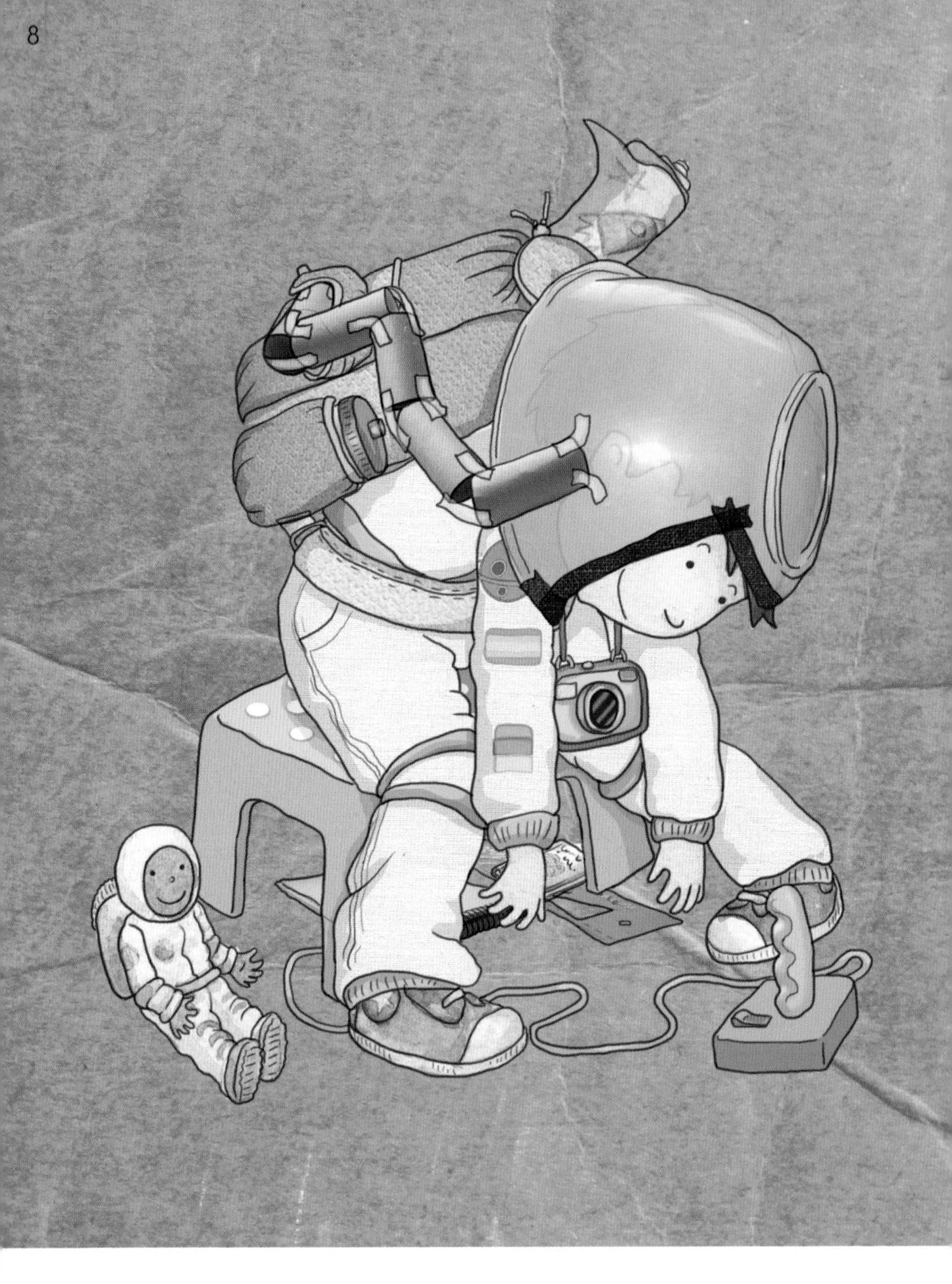

Owen stows his things
below and then he takes his seat.
He furrows his brow

as he looks at the controls.
There's a lot an astronaut
needs to know.

Outside, the crowd cheers.
The engines growl and groan,
3, 2, 1, blastoff!

Inside, Owen and the other astronauts are thrown back against **their** seats as they are blown into space.

Owen looks out the window and calculates how far they have flown.

They have reached a great dark shadow, the black hole.

There is only a narrow entrance to the black hole.

Owen aims the ship, and
they are thrown inside.

Inside the black hole is a tunnel. They see swirling **colors** of red, gold, brown, and yellow.

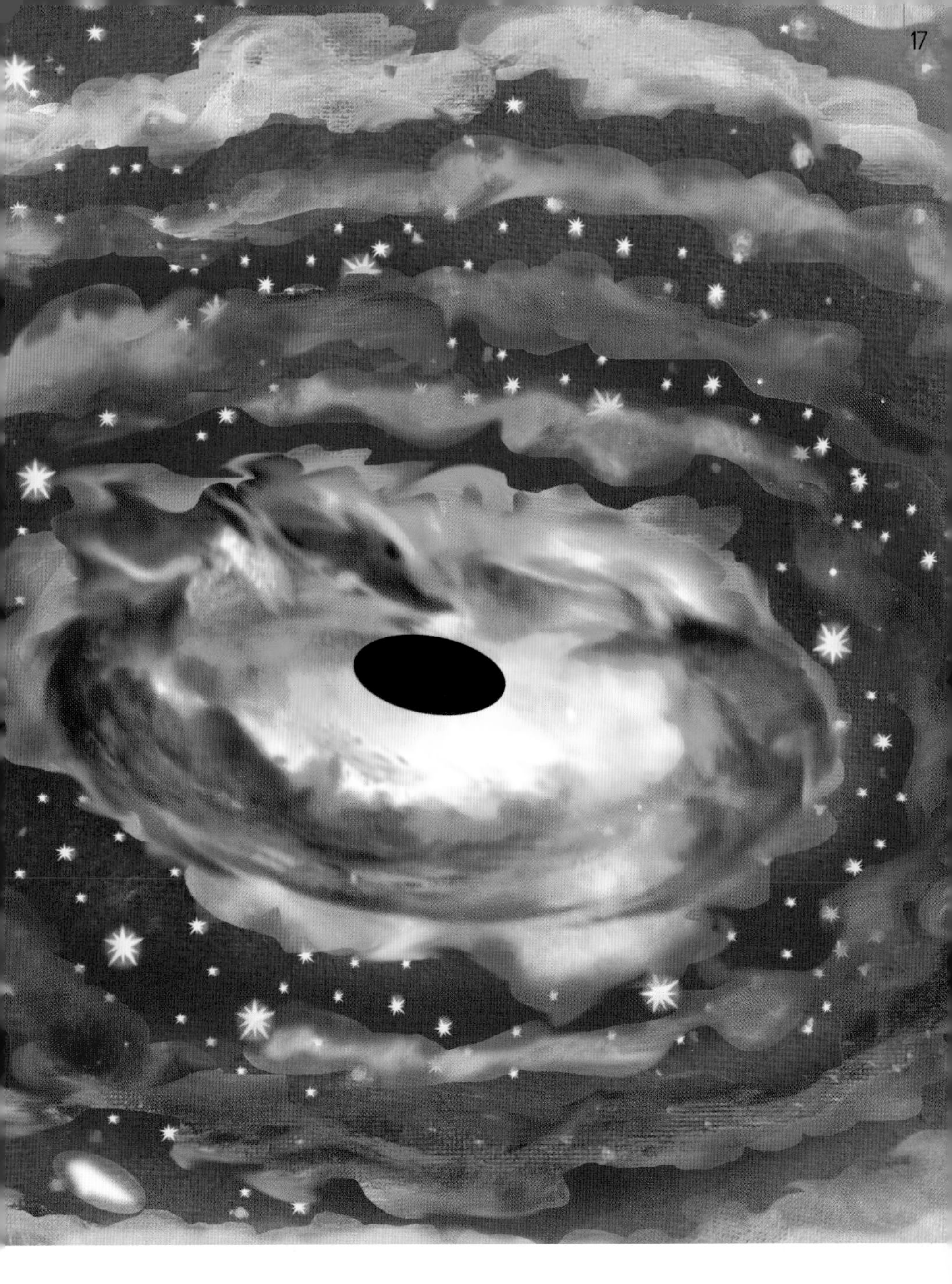

Owen takes a picture.
The tunnel grows more
narrow. Oh no!

Owen grabs the controls
and sharply turns the

spaceship around,
zooming for the exit.

They are thrown back again,
as they are blown out of
the black hole.

Phew!
Owen and his astronauts
have seen the unknown.

They look at the
amazing **pictures**

and head for
home, far below.

OVER 48 TITLES IN SIX LEVELS

Betty Franchi recommends...

Some titles from Level 4

978 1 84898 783 8

978 1 84898 784 5

978 1 84898 785 2

Some titles from Level 5

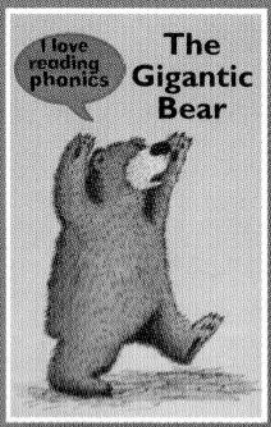

978 1 84898 787 6

978 1 84898 788 3

978 1 84898 789 0

Other titles to enjoy from Level 6

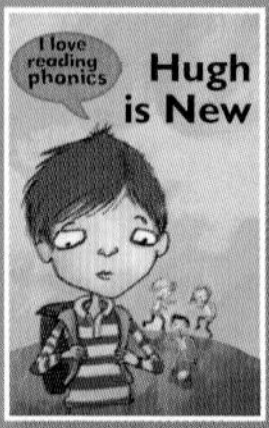

978 1 84898 791 3

978 1 84898 792 0

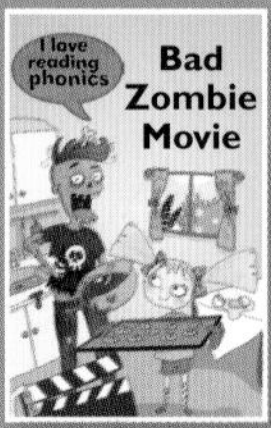

978 1 84898 793 7

An Hachette Company
First published in the United States by TickTock, an imprint of Octopus Publishing Group.
www.octopusbooksusa.com

Distributed in the US by
Hachette Book Group USA
237 Park Avenue, New York NY 10017, USA

Distributed in Canada by
Canadian Manda Group
165 Dufferin Street, Toronto, Ontario, Canada M6K 3H6

ISBN 978 1 84898 794 4

Printed and bound in China
10 9 8 7 6 5 4 3 2 1